Critical Praise for *GraceLand* by Chris Abani

- Winner: 2005 Hemingway/PEN Prize
- Winner: 2005 Silver Medal, California Book Awards
- Winner: 2005 Hurston/Wright Legacy Award
- Finalist: 2005 *Los Angeles Times* Book Prize
- Shortlisted for the Best Book Category (Africa Region) of the Commonwealth Writer's Prize
- 25 Best Books of 2004: *Los Angeles Times*
- Best Books of 2004: *San Francsico Chronicle*
- Barnes and Noble Discover Great New Writers Selection
- *New York Times Book Review* Summer 2004 "Vacation Reading/Notable Books" Selection

"Extraordinary . . . This book works brilliantly in two ways. As a convincing and unpatronizing record of life in a poor Nigerian slum, and as a frighteningly honest insight into a world skewed by casual violence, it's wonderful . . . And for all the horrors, there are sweet scenes in *GraceLand* too, and they're a thousand times better for being entirely unsentimental . . . Lovely."
—*New York Times Book Review*

"Chris Abani's *GraceLand* is a richly detailed, poignant, and utterly fascinating look into another culture and how it is cross-pollinated by our own. It brings to mind the work of Ha Jin in its power and revelation of the new."
—T. Coraghessan Boyle, author of *Drop City*

"Abani's intensely visual style—and his sense of humor—convert the stuff of hopelessness into the stuff of hope."
—*San Francisco Chronicle*

"*GraceLand* amply demonstrates that Abani has the energy, ambition, and compassion to create a novel that delineates and illuminates a complicated, dynamic, deeply fractured society."

—*Los Angeles Times*

"A wonderfully vivid evocation of a youth coming of age in a country unmoored from its old virtues . . . As for the talented Chris Abani, his imaginary Elvis is as memorable as the original."

—*Chicago Tribune*

"*GraceLand* teems with incident, from the seedy crime dens of Maroko to the family melodramas of the Oke clan. But throughout the novel's action, Abani keeps the reader's gaze fixed firmly on the detailed and contradictory cast of everyday Nigerian life. Energetic and moving . . . Abani [is] a fluid, closely observant writer."

—*Washington Post*

"Abani has written an exhilarating novel, all the more astonishing for its hard-won grace and, yes, redemption."

—*Village Voice*

"Ambitious . . . a kind of small miracle."

—*Atlanta Journal-Constitution*

"It is to be hoped that Mr. Abani's fine book finds its proper place in the world . . . [Abani's] perception of the world is beyond or outside the common categories of contemporary fiction and he is able to describe what he perceives compellingly and effectively . . . [Abani captures] the awful, mysterious refusal of life's discrete pieces to fit."

—*New York Sun*

"An intensely vivid portrait of Nigeria that switches deftly between rural and urban life."

—*Boston Globe*

"Singular . . . Abani has created a charming and complex character, at once pragmatic and philosophical about his lot in life . . . [and] observes the chaotic tapestry of life in postcolonial Africa with the unjudging eye of a naïve boy."

—*Philadelphia Inquirer*

"Abani masterfully gives us a young man who is simultaneously brave, heartless, bright, foolish, lustful, and sadly resigned to fate. In short, a perfectly drawn adolescent . . . Abani's ear for dialogue and eye for observation lend a lyrical air . . . In depicting how deeply external politics can affect internal thinking, *GraceLand* announces itself as a worthy heir to Chinua Achebe's *Things Fall Apart*. Like that classic of Nigerian literature, it gives a multifaceted, human face to a culture struggling to find its own identity while living with somebody else's."

—*Minneapolis Star-Tribune*

"*GraceLand* is an invaluable document."

—*San Diego Union-Tribune*

"Remarkable . . . Chris Abani's striking new novel, *GraceLand*, wins the reader with its concept—an Elvis impersonator in Nigeria—and keeps him with strong storytelling and characterization . . . *GraceLand* marks the debut of a writer with something important to say."

—*New Orleans Times-Picayune*

Becoming Abigail

Becoming Abigail

a novella by

Chris Abani

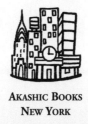

AKASHIC BOOKS
NEW YORK

Published by Akashic Books
©2006 Chris Abani

ISBN-13: 978-1-888451-94-8
ISBN-10: 1-888451-94-7
Library of Congress Control Number: 2005934817

Cover photo by Pierre Bonnard, ©2005 Artists Rights Society (ARS), New York/ADAGP, Paris

Second printing
Printed in Canada

Akashic Books
PO Box 1456
New York, NY 10009
Akashic7@aol.com
www.akashicbooks.com

Also by Chris Abani

Novels
Masters of the Board

GraceLand

Poetry
Kalakuta Republic

Daphne's Lot

Dog Woman

Hands Washing Water

For Blair.

And my nieces: Chinwendu, Nkechi, Natasha, Ibari, and Kelechi.

Lay It As It Plays

I

And this.

Even this. This memory like all the others was a lie. Like the sound of someone ascending wooden stairs, which she couldn't know because she had never heard it. Still it was as real as this one. A coffin sinking reluctantly into the open mouth of a grave, earth in clods collected around it in a pile like froth from the mouth of a mad dog. And women. Gathered in a cluster of black, like angry crows. Weeping. The sound was something she had heard only in her dreams and in these moments of memory—a keening, loud and sharp, but not brittle like the screeching of glass or the imagined sound of women crying. This was something entirely different. A deep lowing, a presence, dark and palpable, like a shadow emanating from the women, becoming a thing that circled the grave and the mourners in a predatory manner before rising up to the brightness of the sky and the sun, to be replaced by another momentarily.

Always in this memory she stood next to her father, a tall whip of blackness like an undecided but upright cobra. And he held her hand in his, another lie. He was silent, but tears ran down his face. It wasn't the tears that bothered her. It was the way his body shuddered every few moments. Not a sob, it was more like his body was struggling to remember how to breathe, fighting the knowledge that most of him was riding in that coffin sinking into the soft dark loam.

But how could she be sure she remembered this correctly? He was her father and the coffin held all that was left of her mother, Abigail. This much she was sure of. However, judging by the way everyone spoke of Abigail, there was nothing of her in that dark iroko casket. But how do you remember an event you were not there for? Abigail had died in childbirth and she, Abigail, this Abigail, the daughter not the dead one, the mother, was a baby sleeping in the crook of some aunt's arm completely unaware of the world.

She looked up. Her father stood in the doorway to the kitchen and the expression she saw on his face wasn't a lie.

"Dad," she said.

He stood in the doorframe. Light, from the outside security lights and wet from the rain, blew in. He swallowed and collected himself. She was doing the dishes buried up to her elbows in suds.

"Uh, carry on," he said. Turning abruptly, he left.

The first time she saw that expression she'd been eight. He had been drinking, which he did sometimes when he was sad. Although that word, sad, seemed inadequate. And this sadness was the memory of Abigail overwhelming him. When he felt it rise, he would drink and play jazz.

It was late and she should have been in bed. Asleep. But the loud music woke her and drew her out into the living room. It was bright, the light sterile almost, the same florescent lighting used in hospitals. The furnishing was sparse. One armchair with wide wooden arms and leather seats and backrest, the leather fading and worn bald in some spots. A couple of beanbags scattered around a fraying rug, and a room divider sloping on one side; broken. Beyond the divider was the dining room. But here, in the living room, under the window that looked out onto a hill and the savanna sloping down it, stood the record player and the stack of records. Her father was in the middle of the room swaying along to "The Girl from Ipanema," clutching a photograph of Abigail to his chest. She walked in and took the photograph from his hands.

"Abigail," he said. Over and over.

"It's all right, Dad, it's just the beer."

"I'm not drunk."

"Then it's the jazz. You know it's not good for you."

But she knew this thing wasn't the jazz, at least not the way he had told her about it on other countless drunken nights. That jazz, she imagined, was something you find down a dark alley taken as a shortcut, and brushing rain from your hair in the dimness of the club found there, you hear the singer crying just for you, while behind her a horn collects all the things she forgot to say, the brushes sweeping it all up against the skin of the drum. This thing with her father, however, was something else, Abigail suspected, something dead and rotting.

"Shhh, go to bed, Dad," she said.

He turned and looked at her and she saw it and recognized what it was. She looked so much like her mother that when he saw her suddenly, she knew he wanted her to be Abigail. Now she realized that there was also something else: a patience, a longing. The way she imagined a devoted bonsai grower stood over a tree.

Now & Then

Now

II

She thought it might rain but so far it hadn't and though a slight breeze ruffled the trees, it wasn't cold. Even down here on the embankment, the night was as crisp and clear as a new banknote. She suddenly wished she had seen a London fog, the kind she had read about; a decent respectable fog that masked a fleeing Jack the Ripper or hid Moriarty from Sherlock's chase. She stopped walking. She was here.

The sphinxes faced the wrong way, gazing inward contemplatively at Cleopatra's Needle rather than outward, protectively, but Queen Victoria had ruled against the expense of correcting the mistake. The obelisk, an Egyptian souvenir, had been a gift from Mohammed Ali. She wasn't sure who he was, but she was pretty sure he wasn't the boxer. Abigail looked at the cold smiles of the sphinxes. Like them, she was amused at the ridiculous impotence of the phallus they stared at. A time capsule was buried beneath the stone tumescence containing, among other things, fashion photos of the most beautiful women of the nineteenth century.

She stood gazing out at the dark cold presence of the Thames. Breaking open a packet of cigarettes she fumbled clumsily to light one. She didn't smoke. With her first drag she imagined she could see the ghosts of those who had also ended it here. At the Needle. Suddenly afraid she smothered a sob, choking on the harshness of the tobacco, eyes tearing. Like the loss of her virginity.

None of the men who had taken her in her short lifetime had seen her. That she wore bronze lipstick, or had a beautiful smile that was punctuated perfectly by dimples. That she plaited her hair herself, into tight cornrows. That her light complexion was a throwback from that time a Portuguese sailor had mistaken her great-grandmother's cries.

None of them noticed the gentle shadow her breasts cast on her stomach as she reached on tiptoe for the relief of a stretch. Never explored the dip in her lower back where perspiration collected like gentle dew. They never weighed the heft of her breast the way she did, had, from the moment of her first bump. Sitting in her room, the darkness softened by a tired moon straining through dirty windows, she had rolled her growing breast between her palms like dough being shaped for a lover's bread. This wasn't an erotic exercise, though it became that, inevitably. At first it was a curiosity, a genuine wonder at the burgeoning of a self, a self that was still Abigail, yet still her. With the tip of a wax crayon she would write "me," over and over on the brown rise of them. And when she washed in the shower the next day, the color would bleed, but the wax left a sheen, the memory of night and her reclamation. But not the men in her life; they hadn't really stopped long enough. She was a foreign country to them. One they wanted to pass through as quickly as possible. None of them knew she had cracked her left molar falling out of a mango tree like a common urchin. Or that in his fear for her safety and the shame of her tomboy nature, her father beat her. Nor did they know that since then, the lushness of mangoes stolen and eaten behind sacks of rice in the storeroom brought her a near sexual release.

But then neither had she really seen them. She tried to. Staring. Watching from the corner of her eye. Trying to piece them together. But they gave nothing, these men. They were experts at hiding themselves, the details of their lives. Even when they walked hand in hand with her in public, it was never the luxuriating of one person in the presence of an equal. No. They led her, pulled her behind their chest-thrust-forward-see-how-lucky-I-am-to-get-such-a-pretty-young-thing walk. They never undressed with her, or for her. There was always a furtive shame to their nudity, and a need to be done quickly, to hide it, theirs and hers, behind clothes again. And this thing that was shameful about them, they put on her, into her, made hers. They left her holding it, like the squish of a tree slug in the mouth, slimy and warm. Something you wanted to spit out and yet swallow at the same time. And though there had only been a few men, sometimes she felt like there had been whole hordes.

She had been ten when her first, fifteen-year-old cousin Edwin, swapped her cherry for a bag of sweets. The caramel and treacle was the full measure of his guilt. Then while stroking her hair tenderly, he whispered softly.

"I will kill you if you tell anyone."

Then

III

And even light can become dirty, falling sluggish and parchment-yellow across a floor pitted by hope walked back and forth, the slap of slipper on concrete echoing the heat gritting its teeth on the tin roof, the sound sometimes like rain, other times like the cat-stretch of metal expanding and contracting.

And there was also the business of reading maps. Her favorite thing. The only things she read. Other than old Chinese poetry in translation. Fragments, memorized, came to her. Mostly from Emperor Wu of Han. Dripping melancholy and loss; she couldn't get enough. The poem: *Autumn Wind . . . I am happy for a moment/ And then the old sorrow comes back/ I was young only a little while/ And now I am growing old/ . . .*

She was lying face down over a large map spread out on the living room floor, studying it intently. She ran her fingers meditatively over the spine of the Himalayas, while peering at the upside-down fish that was New Zealand. There was something in the way the Amazon basin curled up, all green and fresh like a new fern unfurling, that reminded her of a story she had read somewhere about a Chinese poet from a long time ago who tried to live his entire life as a poem.

He was famous for the beautiful landscapes he created in low wide-lipped terra-cotta pots—white sand flowing like a bleached sea floating over the loam holding it up, sweeping up to the miniature trees that would inspire the later Japanese bonsai, rocks lounging in the shade, and little pools with the littlest fish. At least that's what she imagined. There were no pictures to go by, nothing but what her mind could conceive. But it was the story of how he made his tea that stayed with her. Came flooding back as her hands roamed over the smooth green of the map. She mentally went through the process, making a love of it, measured in objects.

An intricate box made from rice paper that allowed just the right amount of air through, held up by a copper handle; and inside, a shallow pot with a lotus in the center. Then at dusk, the freshest tips of green tea picked and wrapped in the petals of the rare blue lotus from Egypt. The box, hung from the rafters of his veranda, took in all that was night. Dawn: the box taken down; the wait for the lotus petals to unravel slowly with the sun; and a pot of hot water, brought to boil; the leaves, dropped in the pot of water; inhaled, the gentle aroma of green tea, suffused with the longing of lotus.

She liked that. Was like that. Wrapping herself each night in anecdotes about Abigail. Collected until she was suffused with all parts of her. She rolled the map up and snapped an elastic band securely around it. Leaving it in a corner, she crossed a shaft of light from the shutters and cut a swathe through the motes, leaving the room to the silence and the dirty, lazy sunlight.

Now

IV

The cigarette burnt her finger as it smoked down to the filter. She threw it into the river. Following its glowing path, she imagined the hiss of its extinction as it hit the thick wet blackness. Sucking her finger she watched a train rumble across a bridge flickering light from its coaches into the water, back and forth over the Thames, carriages lighting the darkness of warehouses and tired stations. It was like the reassurance of blood. That life would go forwards and backwards, but never stop. Not unless the tracks were snowed over.

She pulled up her left sleeve and absently traced the healed welts of her burning. They had the nature of lines in a tree trunk: varied, different, telling. Her early attempts were thick but flat noodles burned into her skin by cashew sap. With time came finer lines, from needles, marking an improvement. But there were also the ugly whip marks of cigarette tips. Angry. Impatient. And the words: *Not Abigail. My Abigail. Her Abigail? Ghosts. Death. Me. Me. Me. Not. Nobody.* She stared at them.

This burning wasn't immolation. Not combustion. But an exorcism. Cauterization. Permanence even. Before she began burning herself she collected anecdotes about her mother and wrote them down in red ink on bits of paper which she stuck on her skin, wearing them under her clothes; all day. Chafing. Becoming. Becoming and chafing, as though the friction from the paper would abrade any difference, smooth over any signs of the joining, until she became her mother and her mother her. But at night, in the shower, the paper would dissolve like a slow lie, the red ink, warm from the hot water, leaking into the drain like bloody tears. That was when she discovered the permanence of fire.

Fumbling about in her bag, she pulled out her purse. Opening it, she stroked the two photographs in the clear plastic pouch, the faces of the two men she loved. Her father, obsidian almost, scowling at the world. Derek, white, smiling as the sun wrinkled the corners of his eyes.

"I am sorry."

She muttered the mantra repeatedly. Soothing.

It was getting chilly and she wished she was wearing more than a light denim shirt. No point in catching a cold as well, she thought, sniffling unconsciously.

Then

V

She stared at the thin undecided film of foam coating the surface of the beer glass on the table. It reminded her of the lake she used to swim in as a child. Not so much a lake, more of a swimming hole; a deep circular cup of rock that sat in the middle of the savanna as though a giant had put down his mug too hard, embedding it in the loose loam. Trees formed a protective circle and birds screamed rudely from the thick foliage.

The beer in the glass sloshed from side to side as she picked it up to clear the dishes from a late reheated dinner served to her father when he got back from the pub, hungry and tired. He had been impatient, making her give him the food near cold. Catching the light, the beer reflected it. The way the swimming hole would: in a bright smile. It reminded her of happier times. That is, until the grief over her mother's death.

It was strange enough just to think about this as grieving. Her mother had died in childbirth—her birth. But this tradition recognized complex ways to be human, and she was allowed to mourn. It was considered harmless. Healing even. The only one who seemed bothered just a little by it was her father. He however deferred to the wisdom of the group and observed silently. Abigail often caught him looking at her and she wondered how it was for him. To watch his child, who looked so much like his dead wife, grieve. As though she was a young version of his wife, grieving her own death in advance.

He was good. Not interfering when she decapitated all her dolls and recreated a funeral for each one. He grew uncomfortable yet still remained silent when she shot six birds from the sky with her rubber catapult and stones collected almost as a meditation from the loose gravel bordering Abigail's grave. He was silent even when she dressed them in lace torn from the trim of her mother's wedding dress. Collecting sticks into bundles that she arranged in geometric patterns, she placed the lace-wrapped birds on these funereal pyres, deliberately holding each one over a candle that stood like a sentinel, until they filled everything with the scent of roasting meat and the revulsion of burning feathers. She took seven photographs of her mother from the family album, tore the faces out and turned them upside down with seven candles on them while she muttered an incantation over the torn faces. Collecting with the deliberateness reserved for communion wafers, she then took the candles off the photo fragments, picked up the fragments, and held the severed photos of her mother's face up to the light before cramming them into her mouth. As he watched her, her father decided that she had crossed the line. She had watched him then with a calm that terrified him, strong even as he unraveled like an untrimmed wick.

The psychiatrist he took her to was overworked and underpaid and only interested in the truly mad. And there were no end of those in their town, wandering the streets naked and sometimes violent, occasionally attacking family members with machetes before settling down to eat the cleaved-off flesh as directed by some unseen deity or demon. The doctor had no time for a mildly confused and lost little girl who he felt just missed her mother, so he prescribed sweet-tasting children's aspirin for her and sent them home.

So her father took her to the local witch. He didn't entirely believe that she was a witch, or that there were real witches. As far as he could tell, she was just an old woman who profited on people's fear. The old witch smiled as she first consulted a spread of cards and then bones and then coins, before telling him to go and buy a heavy silver bracelet and earrings to match, as she needed to use them to anchor the girl in this reality. Reluctantly he did as he was told. As the old woman slipped the jewelry on Abigail, her father asked her if it was necessary.

"Of course it is. You are a man. You know nothing about raising a daughter and buying her nice jewelry."

That memory made her smile and she looked at her

sleeping father almost tenderly. Putting the beer glass and empty dishes in the sink, she returned to wake him to go up to bed. But he looked so peaceful that she left him there on the couch, draping a lappa over him for warmth. As she turned out the lights, she was startled by how clear the moon was. And how beautiful the lone star next to it.

Now

VI

The sound of laughter carried clear across the water and she interrupted her brooding to see a brightly lit party yacht sail past. It was colder now and the water was darker. She longed for some warmth. Another fragment of poetry from Emperor Wu came to her. *From the Most Distant Time/ The years flow like water/ Everything passes away before my eyes.* The lines were loud in her head and a moan escaped her involuntarily. A passing policeman stopped and watched her for a few minutes.

"Are you all right, miss?" he called.

Startled, she dropped the cigarette she was lighting. Picking it up, she nodded. He hesitated, but something about the sphinxes menaced him and he moved on. She looked at the still-glowing tip. She couldn't smoke it now. It had been on the floor. Derek would have smoked it. She smiled as she remembered him. She had only known him for two months, and even then, the actual time spent with him only came to about three and a half weeks, yet she felt like she had known him for much longer. Part of her knew that this was because she brought the intensity of first love to their time.

And she did love him, in spite of his dirty habits. Now, here, she missed them. The way he would pick up food he had dropped, blow it off, and eat it, claiming: "It's still good if it has only been a few seconds." And how he wouldn't always bathe. She knew this because of the way his penis would smell and taste when she rolled back the foreskin. Funky, like old earth: the taste of the loam of her mother's grave. She liked that. I miss him, she thought. *Will* miss him, she corrected. Before the cigarette burned out, she pressed it against her skin. *DSHND*, she wrote. *Death shall have no dominion.* She didn't know where it was from, but Derek liked it. He had showed it to her the first day they met. It was in a book of poems he always carried in his pocket. At least she thought he did. This thing with him was like with her mother. She wasn't always able to tell how much she was inventing and how much was real.

She lit a new cigarette. Sat on the back of the sphinx and watched the traffic wink past. She wondered what the people in their cars, invisible to her, would make of her perched up there, riding the sphinx. Pulling a compact out of her bag, she adjusted her lipstick. One last cigarette, she thought. Not that it mattered at this point.

She coughed through the harsh tobacco, tears stinging

her eyes. The coughing fit caused her to drop her bag and it fell at the foot of the needle, contents spilt: a compact, lipstick, some tissue, a purse, and a book Derek had given her by an African writer, to make her feel at home, he said. The book, *Fragments* by Ayi Kwe Armah, was one of his favorites, he said. She wasn't sure if he meant from Africa or in general. Back then those details didn't matter; now she wished she had asked. Staring at the purse and its contents, she made no move to retrieve them, looking away instead to the river, as the poetry grew louder in her head, forcing its way out of her mouth.

"... *Think of the days/ When we were happy together/,*" she quoted from Su Wu's poem. "*If I live I will come back/ If I die, remember me always/*"

Then

VII

An abandoned truck filled the frame of her window. It had been there since she was a child and she couldn't remember to whom it had belonged. Green moss grew over the left side and bougainvillea draped down from an adjacent building to stroke it in the evening breeze; purple flowers against the burn of rust.

A shrub grew out of the truck's roof, rising straight up from the floor of the cab like an impatient passenger. Birds nested in its open trunk and, judging from the noises issuing from it at dusk, it was home to other creatures too.

Grass grew thick around its wheels and you could almost imagine that they were a pit crew eagerly changing tires. That was the way it was here sometimes. A thing was left where it broke and the land, the forest, soon claimed it back, giving it new meaning, until one day you simply forgot that it was the rusting carcass of a once red truck.

And yet even staring out at that truck, thoughts of Abigail filled her world. By all accounts she had been a tall, thin woman whose eyes held a power beyond the black pools of her irises. Tall, thin, and dark, she, this Abigail, looked so much like the other that her father had named her the same. She was more ghost than her mother, however, moving with the quality of light breathing through a house in which the only footprints in the dust were those of her dead mother. Even her laughter, at once wild and reigned in, was all Abigail.

It remained unspoken between her and her father, but as with all silences, it had all the well-worn familiarity to it of an over-loved pet, shedding fur everywhere it went, leaving faint traces of its animal scent on the hands. And always in that smell, the possibility of danger, of an edge untamed, like a knife unseen in the suds of a washbasin, nicking a finger painfully. Yes, this thing was like that. The shadows under the smiling eyes that said over and over—you killed her. You. Why her? I loved her.

So she was always Abigail. Yet not. How could she be? How could she live up to the reputation of a woman who was known to confront wife beaters and explain to them, quietly and politely, that if they didn't change she would cut off their penises? A woman who was feared by most men for her independent spirit; who at thirty-five became a judge, and set up the first free women's advocacy group. The shape of that Abigail was so clearly marked, the limits traced out in the stories that filled the world around this Abigail, that it was hard to do anything but try to fill the hollowed-out shape.

Insatiable for her mother, she would seek out anyone who had known Abigail and offer to trade a chore for an anecdote, trying to create memory, make it concrete, physical. She collected vignettes about Abigail, hoarding them fiercely. Then late at night, when all was silent apart from the occasional call of night birds and dogs baying at the moon, she would unwrap them in her mind and feast, gorging herself. Sated, she traced their outlines on her skin with soft fingers, burning them in with the heat of her loss, tattooing them with a need as desperate as it was confused. She tried to talk to her father about this need to see herself, but he couldn't understand what she meant. Or maybe he just pretended not to. The desire to be noticed for herself didn't go away though. She couldn't be the ghost he wanted her to be.

One night, she dyed her hair a bright purple and slapped a thick coat of makeup on, before approaching him as he sat in the kitchen at the old table. The wood was worn and nearly white from all the scrub-downs with warm water and abrasive natural soap. There were knife marks, as fine as paper cuts, in the top. She ran her fingers along them meditatively as she sat down at the other end of the table, opposite him. Some of the cuts she recognized, others she didn't. Perhaps Abigail had put them there as she cooked dinner for him. Abigail, this Abigail, hated cooking and was surprised to hear that her independent and fierce mother had still found it in her to tend to her husband in this way. Looking up, her father smiled.

"Hey, baby, can I get you anything?" he asked.

"No, Dad, I just wanted to talk."

"What about?" he asked, folding the newspaper he had been reading into a neat square, which he placed on the table, under the beer mug he had been drinking from. He hadn't been back from work that long and hadn't made it to the bedroom to change.

"About my period," Abigail began. "About being a woman."

He looked away uncomfortably. "Abigail! How can you bring that up, eh? I was just about to ask you to make dinner."

"But Dad."

"Your mother would never have talked like this, you know? She knew the right way to conduct herself," he said. Then, noticing her hair for the first time, he let out a long sigh. "What have you done to your hair? What have I done to deserve this? And why are you wearing all that makeup?"

"What do you care!"

"Abigail!"

"Which one, Dad?"

"What do you mean?"

"This is me, Dad. Me!"

"I know that. How could I not?" he asked. "You look just like your mother. Now, how about making dinner while I go and change?"

The chair made a scraping sound when he pushed back from the table and stood up. As he left the room, he patted her arm and smiled.

It happened while she was cooking. She looked up and out of the window over the sink. In the soft light of dusk she saw a stranger's face reflected back at her: a full head of hair, mascaraed eyelashes, and a red gash of a mouth. She was so shocked she dropped the plate she was washing.

"Are you all right?" her father called out.

"Fine," Abigail mumbled, reaching for the sharp paring knife in the ornately carved wooden rack by the side of the sink. Grabbing a fistful of her hair, she hacked it off. She kept hacking, the hair piling up by her feet, until she had a rough crew cut. Then, reaching into the cupboard above her head, she took out her mother's set of ten glass dishes with lids and placed them carefully on the table.

Rushing upstairs, she grabbed a tampon, some cherry red lipstick, a pair of frilly panties, nail polish, and a picture of Tom Cruise torn out of a magazine. Returning to the kitchen, she put each of the items into a separate dish and covered it. Then she put some locks of her hair into another, some whole dried chilies into another, rice, a washing glove, and nail clippings that looked like drops of dried blood into the last one. Then she arranged the dishes on the kitchen table in a pyramid. When he came down for dinner a few minutes later, her father took in her wild look and the insane display on the table. He looked all crumpled and creased like an empty cigarette packet.

"Those were your mother's marriage dishes," he said finally, as though this desecration was too much.

Now

VIII

Of course she realized that there was the flow and the intent, hers and the river's, and that no amount of thought, or nostalgia, could change this thing at the center of her desire. And how many ways can you describe a landscape? As though the quantities would somehow add up to a math of possibility, a chance even. But such things lay in the realm of luck and were available only to horses and their antagonists.

The neon tower of the Haywood Gallery flashed at her from across the water, part of the ugly South Bank Arts complex. It had never looked so beautiful. The millennium wheel, or the London Eye as it had been officially christened, sat dark and towering like a birthday wish grown too big and abandoned by some child.

She and Derek had taken a ride down the river to Greenwich, from the pier less than five minutes up river, near the cart that sold plastic scale models of The Needle and the sphinxes. They ignored the tour guide's monologue, just happy to be together in the incredible joy of a spring day. Getting off at Greenwich, they explored the Cutty Sark. The cutter, retired from its days as a trade ship carrying spices and tea between India and London, was now a museum. They had stumbled into each other in the narrow gangways giggling like a pair of school kids. Derek led her through the magic of Greenwich's famous market, every bit as romantic as an Arabian souk. Carefully, as if more rode on the decision than was visible, Derek chose an antique-looking silver necklace with a large amber pendant. Against the old tarnished silver, the amber looked like a blob of honey melting on dirty ice. She let him put the necklace on her and lead her up through Greenwich Park, past trees that looked older than the ghost stories they had spun, up the hill to the observatory. Below them, on a clear summer's day, the river and London were visible for miles, he told her, as he pointed away to the distance.

She stood on the line that cut the earth into two time zones, feet inches apart, marveling at how true to life it all was. That one could be only a small step away from another world, another time, and yet caught firmly in one or the other, or as in her case, trapped forever between two. The graffiti, painted and scratched into the wall that curved around the flow of the faded copper line set into the dirt, surprised her, though she couldn't say why. He kissed her then and looked into her eyes with an infinite sadness.

"I'm sorry," he whispered.

Cupping his big face between her small hands, a pair of rare, black butterflies sitting on an outcrop of chalk, she said: "No, no."

He just smiled and rubbed the amber pendant around her neck as though it held the promise of a genie, or as if he were trying to erase something. And they walked through the green of the park. What they walked up was more a rise than a hill, a gentle bumping in the ground. Not unlike what she felt for him: an unassuming tenderness.

Like what she had felt for her father. At least before he died. Before his daily ride on Abigail's coffin became permanent. The rope he had hung himself from, cut, dropped him, not back into this world, but through the floor, and it seemed as though the hard of concrete yielded like the soft of loam. She hadn't cried then, feeling instead his release. And now here he was again, in this stranger's tender fumbling. She touched his face: Derek's. Beneath them the lights of Greenwich flowed into the lights from the Queen's house, running into the Thames. She shivered and he mistook the intent.

"Don't be afraid," he said.

She smiled in the dark and pulled him close. They stood there awhile. Then she unbuttoned his shirt and hers. Her breasts, her nipples hard, pressed into his softer chest. This feeling wasn't the familiarity she had expected. Instead she felt passion enveloping her, and she gave into the safety, the warmth, looking up into his eyes, eyes blue as the sea she had never seen except on television, eyes looking at her, wanting no more than was here. This was love? To be seen. No turning away. No turning toward. Just there.

Later that night, in Derek's home, while his wife slept in their floral wallpapered bedroom under the warmth of bedclothes, they made love on the sofa. And Abigail was giving. For the first time, she wasn't taken. And she wept for her joy and for the loss of Derek's wife upstairs dreaming the dreams of love amidst all that floral wallpaper, as though in an English country garden. Abigail, this Abigail, only this Abigail, always this Abigail, felt herself becoming, even in this moment of taking. Later, as Derek dozed on the sex-rank sofa, stained with their smeared secretions, she stole into the kitchen and finding the needle Derek's wife used to sew all her love into the turkey at Christmas, she held it over the naked flame of the gas range. And in the cold reflection of the microwave's window, she burned two points onto her breasts, one on each. Each one. One on one. Then one in the middle, the hard of her sternum pressing back against the needle. One on her stomach. On each thigh. Each knee. Several round each ankle until they were wearing a garland. Then in the blindness of faith, dots on the back of her thighs, running desperately up to the rise of her buttocks. Then one on her pudenda, dead center. Her fingers followed the needle's point, popping each blister as it rose in heat, as it rose in its hot desire, like dough rising to the love of the flame, rising to the need of the bread, to the unspoken desire of a child in the blue light of predawn hugging the warmth of a loaf against the cold. And each bubble of hope wept salty water running cool and delicious in its sting. And in the tears running down her face she tasted herself for the first time. For the first time tasting the end.

And when she returned to the sofa, he was sitting up smoking, each flare in the dark punctuating his waiting. Sitting, she took the cigarette from him and smoked it. He ran his hands over her, stopping as his fingers encountered the bubbles of Braille. He bent and looked closer, looked at her. She caught his eye and pulled back into the shadows. She knew this look. This wasn't the look in the park. This was the familiar look of men wanting her to be something they wanted.

"What is this?" and his voice carried all the fear of one losing himself in the salt of a woman.

She held his fingers against her. Against her dots.

"This one," she said, touching the ones on each breast, first one, then the other. "This one is you, this, me. In the middle is Greenwich. Here," and she was down on her stomach, "is my hunger, my need, mine, not my mother's. And here, and here and here and here, here, here, here, me, me, me. Don't you see?" and she showed him the words branded in her skin. How had he missed them when they made love? But he had. "This is my mother," she was saying. "This is my mother. Words. And words. And words. But me? These dots. Me, Abigail."

And he traced her in that moment, the map of her, the skin of her world, as she emerged in pointillism. Emerging in parts of a whole. Each. Every. He wondered what would form should he draw a line between each dot. Connecting. And what would he use for ink? Blood? Semen? He held her. Held her and cried. While upstairs his wife slept. Held her, this man-child who was her social worker.

His tears felt cool on the hot of her skin. And she smiled as his release cooled her. Like finely worked metal. And she smiled. In the dark.

Standing here, now, at The Needle, face turned to Greenwich as if seeing the memories play against the dark sky, she rubbed the amber pendant still around her neck furiously. There was nothing more that could be done. Now that she had been found she realized the deeper joy was to be lost. And the amber pendant burned a deeper dot, a deeper mark, invisible though it was. No, the deeper joy wasn't being lost. But it wasn't being found. It was being seen. And now that she could not feel that gaze on her, she was more lost than ever.

"Abigail," she called softly to the dark. The cold. The water. "Abigail."

And with the hum of traffic behind her, it was as though she hadn't spoken.

As if the wind was merely passing through her.

Then

IX

She was in a bus on her way home from school. Early. Her cousin Peter was home from London and her father had sent for her. She already knew why. Something lying in the middle island of the freeway caught her eye, diverting her attention. It looked to her like the body of a baby, perhaps tossed from the window of a speeding car by a teenage mother unable to cope. It wasn't an unusual thought in this country where the dead littered the streets of big towns and cities like so much garbage. But as they drew closer it was simply an untidy pile of rubber from a blown tire. Even though she knew it wasn't the corpse of a baby, somehow the thought of death stayed with her. It should have been an omen, especially on this day, when she knew Peter and her father were talking about her going back to London with him.

Thinking of London and her cousin Peter reminded her of her father's funny stories about his time there. He seldom told them because it invariably meant talking about Abigail. They had gone together. In 1950. Once or twice, though, he would share a story. Like the time he had gone round to look at a bedsit to rent. Not much more than a room with an oil stove for cooking and warmth.

White landlords, reluctant to rent to blacks, put up signs that read: *No Blacks. No Irish. No Dogs.* So he had been careful on the telephone when he called up, speaking in the most modulated accent he could summon, somehow managing to pass. He was counting on it being harder for the landlady to turn him down if he and Abigail were standing on the front step.

They arrived promptly at four p.m. as asked and stood clammy hand in clammy hand while they waited for the landlady to answer the bell. It was winter and the street lamps were already on to light the darkness that had fallen suddenly and densely at three. Her father cleared his throat and smiled reassuringly at Abigail as they heard footsteps approach the door. It swung open to reveal a white woman of indeterminate age—she could have been anywhere between fifty and seventy. She took in the grinning black faces on her stoop and with a short scream fell into a faint.

Terrified that she had died of a heart attack and that they would be held responsible, they took off at a fast trot down the street and didn't stop for a good mile. Of course, he was laughing as he told her the story, and Abigail laughed along, imagining her mother and father running down a winter-dark London street. But she could still see the sadness haunting the corners of his eyes, and she was unsure if it was for Abigail, the humiliation of that day, or both.

When she arrived home after the bus ride, he was sitting on the front veranda supervising Anwara, the local carpenter, who was building a small house. That had been four years before, when she was just ten.

"What is it, Dad?" she asked as she fetched him a cup of cold water.

He accepted it gratefully and drank it in one long gulp. Snapping the dregs to the floor with one fluid arm movement, he asked her to fetch another one for Anwara before he answered. She did, and as Anwara drank, she walked back to her father.

"So what is he building? A dollhouse?"

"A dollhouse, humm?" he replied. "No, darling, it is a doghouse."

"A doghouse?" she asked, surprised. She had never heard of a doghouse and had really hoped it was a dollhouse for her. What did Pedro, their three-legged dog, need a house for anyway? He had slept on the veranda under her father's chair very happily for as long as she could remember. Mistaking her resentment for confusion, he explained how all the dogs in London had doghouses and since Pedro was getting old he thought it might be a good idea to build him some shelter from the elements. She didn't respond and he went on to tell her how women in London sent their husbands to the doghouse if they misbehaved and assured her that as the woman of the house, she could do the same to him. She knew he was joking, but somehow it reassured her. That had been about a month ago. Pedro, however, never took to his new residence, preferring his spot under the chair on the veranda, and so a noisy hen and her brood occupied the doghouse.

Now

X

Sometimes there is no way to leave something behind. Something over. We know this. We know this. We know this. This is the prevalence of ritual. To remember something that cannot be forgotten. Yet not left over. She knew this. As she smoked. She knew this. This. This. This. And what now?

Then

XI

Peter wasn't really her cousin, but was married to her cousin Mary. A few years before, at twelve, Abigail had been a bridesmaid at their wedding. She had loved every minute of it. The ceremony, the flower petals strewn everywhere, even the ugly chiffon dress and having to dance with Uncle Ekwi, who stank of decay in the way even the cleanest old people did.

Peter had cornered her in the bathroom. She didn't shrink away like other girls her age might have at being surprised in the bathroom with her underwear halfway down her legs and the skirt of her dress gathered in a bunch as she squatted over the hole. Nor did she seem impressed that he was a Johnny-just-return. She just held her dress up and peed, not taking her eyes off his. Surprised at her fearlessness he kissed her, his finger exploring her.

Later, when he was back at Mary's side, she caught him

sniffing his finger occasionally, a smile playing around his lips. If she had felt it was anything special, she certainly didn't show it, and in time it simply faded into the distance, like an old wine stain on ivory muslin. Even at that young age she knew what men were like.

She hadn't seen him since that incident, though he returned to the village from London once a year. She had been away at boarding school and so missed him. She might have missed him this time too, had she not transferred to a local school and become a day student because her father had dropped into depression so serious, he needed her to take care of everything for him. His sudden summons had been something of a treat for her, because it signaled an improvement on his part. She was grateful to Peter for that at least.

Peter was apparently a successful businessman in London and was very generous to the villagers when he came home, paying for a hospital bill here, new glasses there, some child's school fees over there, and so forth. Her father really liked him and had often told her about Peter and his trips when she got back from boarding school on breaks.

"He always takes one young relative back to London as well," he used to explain. "Imagine how lucky those children are!"

Now

XII

The dog sniffed at the sphinx. At first, Abigail thought it was unaccompanied. But following closely, at the end of a long red leash, was an old woman. Abigail smiled as the dog lifted its leg and peed on the sphinx. The old woman waited patiently while the dog, a fluffy pink poodle, took care of business. All the while she stared at Abigail, though she said nothing. When the poodle was done, they shuffled past, the old crone and the dog, each leading and following alternately.

Overhead, a plane traced light across the dark. Abigail read in *Reader's Digest* that all plane landings were controlled crashes. Like the way we live our lives, she thought. Bumble through doing the best we can and hoping that some benevolence keeps us from crashing. Lighting another cigarette, she wished the plane bringing her and Peter to London that day had crashed.

She felt a raindrop on her skin and looked up into the

night. She couldn't see any rain clouds and there had been no mention of rain on the weather report. She would have remembered. She always checked the weather before she went out. Smiling to herself, she realized how stupid it was to check the weather before coming here. Another raindrop fell, triggering old memories.

There was a time, it seemed to her, that she lived purely for the pleasure of rain. The way it would threaten the world gently, dropping dark clouds over the brightness of an afternoon, wind whipping trees in dark play. Then the smell; carried from afar, the lushness of wet, moisture-heavy earth, heralding the first cold stabs of water that seemed to just be practicing for the torrent that was about to come. And she, sitting on the dry safety of the veranda, wrapped in a sweater, watching the world weep as the Beatles in the background, tinny and small in the soundscape, asked, *Dear Prudence, won't you come out to play?*

Glancing at the sky worriedly, she wondered if it was really going to rain. So far there had been nothing more than the first few drops. Well, can't worry about that now, she thought, as she lit another cigarette and blew the smoke into the empty eye socket of the sphinx.

Then

XIII

Peter was sitting in her father's favorite chair. An old leather thirties armchair that was comfortable and smelled of the dreams of everyone who had sat in it. She wasn't sure why, but Abigail felt a surge of anger at this when she walked in from school. Her father smiled at her from the sofa and she felt Peter's eyes on her body when she passed by in the short skirt of her uniform. She went upstairs and changed into a pair of sweats. Coming back downstairs, she re-entered the sitting room. A quick glance revealed the men had already helped themselves to beer.

"Are you hungry, Dad?" she asked, pointedly ignoring Peter.

"Abigail, where are your manners? Offer our guest food first," her father replied.

"It's okay," Peter said smiling. "I'm sure she didn't mean anything by it. But thank you for your offer, I am kind of hungry."

Shooting him a look, she went into the kitchen and soon the sound of pots banging carried through to them. In no time at all, she had made a big plate of eba and a steaming bowl of egusi soup.

"Lunch is ready," she called as she set the kitchen table. Bringing their drinks in with them, the two men sat down and looked surprised when she joined them. They had expected her to eat later, or simply take her food to her room, while they discussed important things.

"You're joining us?" her father asked. But it wasn't a question. More a reprimand.

"Yes," she replied.

"That's just fine, because I am here to talk about you," Peter said. "Mary has asked that I bring Abigail back on this trip to come and live with us in London. She can finish school there."

"But my father needs me," she said. "Besides, won't it get crowded with the other relatives you've taken to live with you already?"

Mary needed her, Peter explained. All the other kids he had taken back had fallen in with bad crowds and run away. Abigail's father wanted her to go back with Peter.

"Your life will be better," he said, voice quiet. "London will give you a higher standard of education and living."

She felt his sacrifice knowing that he was fighting his heart the urge to beg her to stay. But there was also the faintest shadow in his eyes, one that revealed rather than occluded. She shivered and crossed herself, arms and legs locked.

Now

XIV

"Dreadful about Chechnya," Abigail repeated over and over as she watched *Bridget Jones's Diary* for the tenth time.

"Dreadful about Chechnya," Abigail said to the sphinx, smiling at the memory. She had been trying to perfect her English accent. She realized pretty quickly, from the way she was treated at the shops and in the doctor's office, that the English could forgive you anything except a foreign accent. The flat was silent other than the contortions of her voice.

She heard the key in the lock and paused the film as Mary came in. Abigail got up to help with the grocery bags. Chatting away in the kitchen as they put away the food, Abigail wondered absently if this was how it would have been if her mother lived. There was comfort in this simple task. The ordering of life in cupboards and refrigerator shelves.

Lingering over a cup of tea made in that special way

(boiled twice in evaporated milk and ginger), she watched Mary, who watched the rain outside. The plastic climbing frame and slide set mourned in a corner of the garden next to the pink and purple Wendy house. Bought for a child who had died. Suddenly. Mysteriously.

"Do you miss her?" Abigail asked.

"All the time," Mary said. Voice. Small. Distant.

"Me too," Abigail said.

Returning to the present, Abigail lit another cigarette against the cold.

"Yeah, me too," she said to the night.

Then

XV

There was a quality of silence. An awe in the face of mountains that had kept their secrets for a millennia. This drew Abigail to maps. Not all maps. Old ones. Printed on paper that was more parchment. Big ones. That unrolled with all the crackling promise of a flying carpet warming up. And lines. Rivers meandering lazily in blues and sometimes silver. Hills rising in red circles, uneven, thick at their bases and thinning toward the top; like balding men. The green ticks of forests and jungles. The brown sprawls of deserts. And the black lines of science, carving things into sections—longitude, latitude—pretending that here, at least, on the flat spread of the map, it was possible to have any kind of dominion over a landscape. Over things.

And sometimes the alchemy of her stare transmuted the parchment into her mother's skin. The landmarks taking on deeper significance. The Himalayas marking the slope of

Abigail's forehead, spreading into the Gobi desert. The hook of Africa became her nose. Australia her bottom lip. And the islands between India and Tasmania became the fragments of teeth bared in a smile. In true cubist form, the Americas were her eyes. Everything else became the imagined contours of her inner life.

This was how Abigail spent many rainy afternoons, the cartographer of dreams. Of ghosts.

Now

XVI

And this was the shape of her desire:

To be a white bird beating its wings against night. Beating until that was all. To be. Yet not the bird. Or night. Or the air. Or the beating.

To be a white bird.

Then

XVII

She had felt caught in the sheath of men's plans. From the time her father and Peter had decided that she needed to come to London. There had been the trip to Lagos in the long lean body of a bus. Then the flight in the cigar belly of the plane, and now, hurtling through the bowels of London in the subway, headed for Peter and Mary's.

She studied the curious map of the London Underground system with interest. It wasn't much good as a map printed the way it was on thick cardboard tacked to the wall opposite. It was nestled between a poem and an advertisement for Cadbury Creme Eggs. She promised herself she would try that as soon as possible. Turning her attention to the poem, she smiled. *To what can our life on earth be likened?/ To a flock of geese,/ alighting on the snow./ Sometimes leaving the trace of their passage?/ Su Shi.* I should burn that onto my arm, she thought, mentally searching to see if she had any room left. These were good omens. The two main things she loved, here, at the moment of her arrival.

The map was a mass of lines—reds, blues, yellows, greens, blacks, browns, and even a deep purple. Laid out the way it was, it made her think London spread out in a neatly laid out geometric square. She would find out later that it was an old and untidy sprawl of rivers and canals, beautiful parks, old cobbled streets that still held the echo of horse drawn carriages, tired crumbling walls built by Caesar, and modern plazas of glass and chrome. There was the open plea-sure of Covent Garden with its flower shops, vegetable stalls, colorful barrow boy calls, the new market with stall after stall selling trinkets that nobody needed to people who should know better. There were street musicians everywhere filling the hallowed halls of the Underground with their melan-cholic worship. But that would come later. With Derek. That and his tongue that filled her with a desire so deep it threatened to rip her apart.

For now there was just the clacky-clack of the tracks, the warm rush of air as they hurtled down one of the city's many arteries, and the swaying that was a lulling to sleep. And the people around, careful to avoid their luggage sitting in the center of the carriage. Eyes never meeting. Reading. Bopping heads to music filtered through headphones. Nodding off to sleep. Packed tightly as they were, she still noticed the small island around everyone. And so many white people. Shades of white. She had never thought of it that way. But it was true. White as translucent as snow, making visible the veins running like green rivers just underneath the skin. Others that were denser, pinker, blood vessels spreading like tentacles of light. Others that seemed unsure whether to be a dirty ivory or a rich cream. And brown ones, tanned deep like the happy flow of a tropical river down a mountainside. She wondered what her mother had made of all these shades.

She studied Peter as he slept. In this moment of vulnerability, nostrils flared in a snore, drooling slightly, he looked like a child. She had been suspicious of him from the beginning. Not just because of what he had done to her when she was twelve, but because there was something about him that didn't ring true. It was as if he hadn't learned to occupy his body properly. Or perhaps it was his life that he hadn't stepped into, occupying instead another one. One that was clearly uncomfortable. It made her uncomfortable that she couldn't place it. Bad people didn't bother her. Like good people they were a known quantity. It wasn't even the loose possibility of these that bothered her. It was the struggle against either side. That was where the danger lay. What was it Abigail used to tell her? A house divided, that's the dangerous place. She smiled suddenly. Abigail couldn't have told her anything. Still, she didn't buy Peter's story about the other kids he took back having run off with bad company. He had done something to them, she didn't know what, but she was going to watch him closely, make sure it didn't happen to her. That was what Abigail would have done. She would have studied Peter's face too in this moment of openness so as not to be taken in by it.

She turned her attention back to the Underground map, mouthing the words of the stops as if they were a mantra that would reveal all to her. She let the vowels and consonants sink to the bottom of her mouth like the pendulous seed of a mango still holding the sweetness of flesh. She then dropped it down one more level and swished the words around the back of her throat as though gargling. Walthamstow. Mornington Crescent. Angel. Highbury & Islington. Finsbury Park. Tottenham Court Road. Oxford Circus. And on. When the train pulled into the lit-up tiled station bearing the legend *Seven Sisters*, Peter woke on cue and gathered the luggage. He stepped off without bothering to check if she was with him. Abigail hesitated at the gap between the door and the platform. In the sliver of darkness she saw a rat moving. It was oddly comforting.

"Come on," Peter said.

"*Seven Sisters. Mind the gap,*" the station announcement said. "*Mind the gap.*"

Now

XVIII

Landscape, in the sense of the sublime, might overwhelm the self.

Of course Abigail didn't think that. Not in those words. As she smoked and squinted into the misty age of the river, the Thames, she thought: Thank God for maps. For a way to hold it all. She wondered how old it was. *Donkey's ears.* She laughed. Mr. Ekwensi, her fifth grade teacher, always said that. *Donkey's ears.* Old as. Why donkey years anyway? She lit another cigarette.

So much of love is memory, she thought, her mind tracing the outline of Derek. She had loved him so completely and he her. But what are the limits of desire? The edges beyond which love must not cross? Those were questions she had heard others discuss in these last few days. Discuss as if she was a mere ghost in their presence. Called this thing between Derek and her wrong. How could it be?

There is only so much we can do to save those we love.

Then

XIX

This was how she found her father. Hanging. The week she was to leave with Peter. Hanging. From the hook where the ceiling fan had been. And now a cruel breeze blew in and he swayed in the raveling and unraveling of the hemp rope. Round. And round. Like a lazy Christmas ornament. And down one leg, and pooling on the floor, his reluctance. Yellow. And in the heat, putrid, rank with him. His life. His loss. And she didn't cry. Didn't seem shocked. Knew. Always knew. It was more a matter of when. And how.

She sat on the floor beneath him. Felt his toe brush her cheek with every turn. Turn by turn. His big toe. Spiced with his urine. And the uncut toenail, rough on her face. Sharp enough to cut. Cut a small line. Line linking her to him. Him held only by that line falling. Falling from the ceiling in hemp. Hemp becoming flesh. Flesh the fluid of him, leaking. Leaking down his leg. Leg ending in the toe. Toe brushing her cheek with a cut. Cut the line. Cut the line. Line. The rope. Rope-saw-rough voices. Voices calling. Falling heavy in the dust around her. Her sitting on the floor. Floor where his crumpled body was laid on the hard of concrete. Concrete falling away into the soft of loam and he falling. Falling into Abigail. Abigail, her, sitting on the floor. Losing him. Him losing her. Her. She. She the reason for him doing this. This love. Love calling to love.

She sitting on the floor. Floor patterned by the footprints of those voices who cut him down. Down from the line. She dipped her finger in the pool of him and brought it to her lips. The salt of him. The sum of him. There is no way to leave anything behind. She soaked her hands in him. Brought them wet and shiny in the sunlight to her face. Smeared. But water is just that. Nothing left behind but the prickle of his evaporation and the faint fragrance of loss. Loss: She knew this. Knew this. Knew this.

This wasn't grief. Grief wasn't the measure. Joy, joy, joy. Shameless. Shameful. Abandoned. Released. She rolled in it. It coated her in liquid and dust. There was no line. Just this wet muddy smudge of him, and the spent form of her.

And she laughed.

Now

XX

What is light?

The blinding of the Thames River Police strobing night and water. Bubbles of light riding the face of dark as the London Eye turned slowly. The people enclosed in the glass jar flickering against the background of light. Imagined laughter, like shadows, shouted across water.

In the scene there was nothing of her reflected. Nothing of her desire. And for this she was grateful because she was no more than a lonely self in dialogue with the dead. To see herself reflected would be to see the dead. Returned. Returning. When the dead do it, it is only despair. And revenge.

When she lit the cigarette.

It was more.

For the light of the match.

She inhaled. She thought:

This is a dark place.

Then

XXI

Peter and Mary fought that night. The night Abigail arrived. The shouting had woken her. She crept out of bed, tiptoeing across the creaking floorboards to stand at the threshold of the door leading into the living room. Down a hallway she could see bedrooms, and at the end, Peter and Mary's. The door was open and she watched them. They stood facing each other like actors in a paused movie. Abigail was caught in a bubble of time and silence, waiting, until: there it was again, the sound that woke her. It was like dry wood cracking, but not loud. It sounded like bones in a knuckle delivering an open backhanded slap. It was the sound of derision, for the softness of flesh, of the heart. That was the weight of the sound. Abigail flinched, her own knuckles clenching tight like a promise bound up in the hardness of bone. Mary didn't move. Just sobbed. Abigail couldn't imagine why Mary would let Peter hit her and not fight back. She was unsure what to do, but knew she had to do something.

They seemed to be arguing about her. From what she could gather, Mary did not want her there, which she found strange as they were really close. Another crack. Peter's second backhand across Mary's face decided it for her. She flew at him, gouging a deep furrow under his eye. He shouted and kicked wildly. One of the kicks caught her in the stomach. Knocking her clear across the room. He snarled at her and stomped off. Mary sobbed as Abigail cradled her, her breath shallow from the hate in her stomach.

"You should not have done that," Mary kept repeating. "Shouldn't have."

A few days after her arrival, Peter took Abigail shopping. The shopping center was bigger than anything she had ever seen, at least in one building. The only thing bigger was the open-air market back home. She rode the escalators with trepidation. And Peter laughed at her. Called her a bush woman. Secretly taking pleasure in her delight at the window displays, and the racks and racks of clothing, and the soft carpets, and the bright lights, and the polite assistants.

If she noticed the disapproving looks the older women gave Peter as he bought her tight, revealing clothes made for women much older, she didn't show it. Finally, he took her to the makeup counter of a store.

"Show her how to make up," he told the assistant. "Show her, and then tell me what to buy."

The assistant, herself no more than twenty, looked confused.

"But sir," she said. "She looks too young."

"That's the problem," he said. "Make her look older than a fourteen-year-old."

Shrugging, the assistant did her work. Showing Abigail how to define her cheek bones with blusher. Brush the kohl-like mascara through her eyelashes. Deepen the dark of her eyebrows. Lift her lips from her face. Abigail leaned back as far as she could without falling out of the high stool. When she was done, both the assistant and Peter stared. Abigail was beautiful. And older.

"She knows how to use it, right?" Peter asked as he paid. The assistant nodded.

Abigail stared at her mother in the mirror.

She smiled.

Later, over a milkshake at McDonald's, lured into safety by Peter's generosity, she asked, "What happened to all of the other kids you took back? I haven't met any."

He smiled, "You'll find out soon."

That night, Peter burst into her bedroom. Late. Abigail started up as though a nightmare was following her into the waking world. Two men stood in the doorway. The hall light fuzzed them into dark-haloed shapes. From the feral breathing and almost soundless smirk she could tell that one of the shapes was Peter. The other was a mystery to her.

"Peter?" she ventured, pushing the bedclothes aside and

making to get up. But it was the other figure that approached her.

"Hello," the voice husked.

"Who are you?" she demanded.

"You don't need to know that," the man said.

He was now standing in front of her. Menacing. She tried to retreat under the bedclothes. He pulled them away. She scuttled back but he grabbed her and pushed his weight onto her. She fought him. Shouting. The sound caught deep in her throat. Calling for Mary. The man was like an incubus. The weight of his lust crushing her. The more she fought the heavier he got.

"Yes," he grunted. "Fight."

"Mary!" she screamed, finally finding her voice.

Mary appeared at the door. Tears washed foundation from her face in brown streaks. They locked eyes: Mary's pleading with her as she stepped back, gently closing the door behind her. Peter smiled triumphantly; turning to the man, he said:

"Fuck her. Fuck her hard."

The weight on top of her stirred excitedly. She closed her eyes and brought her knee up and all the fight went out of him. The man squealed and fell off.

"What! What the fuck!" Peter shouted. He made to slap her, but she caught his hand and bit deep, drawing blood. He yelled and then stepped back. Abigail was standing on the bed, eyes wild, the makeup she had been too excited to take off, smudged. The man on the floor was groaning. Peter helped him up. They retreated. She could hear muffled shouts, doors slamming, and a car starting up. She gave into her trembling and crumpled into the bed, sobbing. She didn't hear the door open. Only felt Peter grab her from behind, forcing her face into the pillow. He handcuffed her. Arms behind her back. Slipped a harness with a ball into her mouth and over her head, chipping her teeth in the process. Grabbing her by the hair, he dragged her out of the bedroom.

"You want to bite like a dog? I'll treat you like a dog."

Abigail struggled as he half-pushed her down the hall and out into the backyard. Mary followed. Crying. Saying his name over. Softly.

"Peter. Peter."

"Shut up or you'll join her!" he screamed, rounding on her. But she was too far gone into whatever trance she was in and just kept repeating, "Peter. Peter."

The ground was cold and wet with dew and frost and Abigail's nightgown was streaked, dirty, by the time he stopped in front of the empty doghouse. He handcuffed her to the chain lying in front of it. She pulled against it. It was firmly embedded in the ground.

"This is what we do to dogs," he said.

He spat at her and she flinched away. He turned to go, then stopped. Pulling his penis out, he peed all over her. Laughing as she thrashed about.

"That's my dirty dog," he said. "Dirty dog."

Then

XXII

And this is how she was made.

Filth. Hunger. And drinking from the plate of rancid water. Bent forward like a dog. Arms behind her back. Kneeling. Into the mud. And the food. Tossed out leftovers. And the cold. And the numbing of limbs that was an even deeper cold.

Without hands, she rooted around her skin with her nose. Feeling for the brandings, for the limits of herself. And then the urge came, and she held it away, held it away. Until she let go, she couldn't feel the warmth wash down the frozen limits of her skin.

Without hands, she bit at the itches from blood vessels dying in the cold. From the intimacy of dirt. Bending. Rooting. Biting. Her shame was complete.

And Peter came every day. Twice a day. At dawn. At dusk. To feed and water her. With rotting food. Rancid water. Sometimes his piss. By the tenth day she no longer cared. Couldn't tell the difference.

And when Peter was out. At work. The angel came. Sometimes it wore the face of Mary's dead daughter. Sometimes Mary's. Told her stories. How Peter had beaten the girl. Just months old. Because she wasn't a boy. Beaten Mary. Until that night. When he threw her down the stairs. She fell on the baby she was holding. How the child died. Accidental, the coroner ruled.

And she wept as Mary warmed her limbs in the electric blanket. How Abigail would follow the red line in the snow. The electric cord becoming the umbilical for a new birth. A divine birth. And Mary's tears would melt the snow. And Abigail would nod and whisper: I know. I know. I know.

And the sound of the words was a hoarse rasp. Formless.

And Mary would echo: I know. I know. I know.

And the sound was a woman crying in the snow. Wrapping her guilt in an electric blanket. Wrapped around a girl slowly becoming a dog.

Now

XXIII

It was all grace.

Jumping down from the sphinx's back, Abigail picked up the contents of her handbag and stuffed them back in. She paused over the book that lay where it had fallen open and she read:

A human being alone is a thing more sad than any lost animal and nothing destroys the soul like aloneness.

She traced the words with the tip of her finger, stopping where the rain had smudged the phrase, *the soul like,* spreading the ink into an angel's wings. She shut the book and opened it again at random. This was an old game she had played with the Bible as a child. To follow the guidance of whatever passage revealed itself. *Fragments* opened at the flyleaf, to Derek's inscription.

Gentle Abigail, This book will show you that even though you come from a dark ~~continent~~ *place, you can escape your fate. Derek.*

Then

XXIV

Fifteen days, passing in the silence of snow.

And she no longer fought when Peter mounted her.

Wrote his shame and anger in her. Until. The slime of it threatened to obliterate the tattoos that made her.

Abigail.

Then

XXV

One night.

Unable to stand it anymore, she screamed. Invoking the spirit of Abigail.

And with her teeth tore off Peter's penis.

Then

XXVI

In the ensuing.

There was no panic. Just the angel unlocking her cuffs. And Peter bleeding. Reddening the snow on this dark and rebellious night. Peter dying.

"Go," the angel said.

"Go," Mary said.

Abigail ran out, half-naked, the severed penis clutched in her hand. Though the streets were crowded, only a few people noticed this gorgon with bloody mouth and hands, and the grisly prize she held up like a torch as she ran.

Time bled into the cracks on the pavement until a passing police car picked her up.

Now

XXVII

From across the water.

It seemed like an endless train was coming, clattering over the rails of Charing Cross Bridge. Sex. That was what trains and tunnels reminded Abigail of. And lust.

She thought of the Igbo name for train. There wasn't one. Or maybe she had just forgotten. She had forgotten so much, lost so much. Derek once asked her what the Igbo word for horizon was.

"I can't remember," she said, wondering how without a name she could describe its curve and keep from falling off the edge of the world. These are the places where desire collects, she thought, lighting another cigarette. She took a handkerchief out of her pocket and blew her nose. She held it there long after she was done. It smelled good. Smelled of Derek. In that moment she felt him rush into her. Following closely after, the voice of an aunt who once told her she left her husband because of how he smelled.

"You can forgive a man a lot," she said. "But not how he smells. The moment you can't stand that, you can't stand the man."

So much lost.

Then

XXVIII

Derek was the social worker who came for her the next morning.

Abigail found it hard to believe that this short balding man could help her in any way. But there was a kindness about him that was reassuring. He sat across from her, blinking rapidly behind his glasses as he read her file. She wondered what was written there. Girl found with penis in hand? Claims to have bitten it off? Was silent, withdrawn, malnourished, with the onset of frostbite, otherwise fine?

"What's your name?" he asked, putting down the file as though he didn't trust it.

She stared at him. Sullen.

"Do you speak English?"

That stung and there was the brief flare of anger in her eyes. He smiled.

"I'm sorry," he said. He had seen it. She was impressed.

Most people she knew never really looked at her.

"Are you thirsty?"

She nodded and he got up and left the room, returning with a cold can of Coca-Cola and a KitKat.

"Where are you from?"

She popped the tab and took a deep drink of the cold soda. Then she ripped the chocolate open and ate quickly, ravenously, noisily.

"Where are you from?" he repeated. His voice was kind. Soothing. Showed no impatience. He took off his glasses and polished them as he waited for her to answer. She played with the empty can. He got up. Left the room. Came back. A second can of Coke. Another KitKat.

"What is your name?" he asked as she ripped into the drink and food.

Finishing, she sat back, belched loudly. He laughed. She smiled.

"Hungry?'

She nodded. He got up. Opened the door.

"Come," he said.

She followed him, through labyrinth corridors, into the belly of the hospital, to a canteen. He gave her a tray and followed with one of his own. He watched her with paternal tenderness as she filled it until there was no more space for food. He paid and followed her lead to a table by a window. Sipping at his tea, his only purchase for himself, he watched her eat. Neither spoke for the half hour it took her to finish the two steak pies, three packets of crisps, a BLT, a plate of

French fries, two cupcakes, and a Chelsea bun. Finishing the second of two cans of ginger ale, she sat back and looked at him for a long time. He had been reading a book of poems and he put it down on the table.

"What are you reading?" she asked.

"Dylan Thomas. You want to hear?" Not waiting for a reply, he read a line, his favorite. *"And death shall have no dominion."*

She nodded. Not Chinese poetry, but not bad, she thought, but said nothing.

"I'm Derek," he said, offering her his hand to shake. She took hold of it, noting its softness, the faint smell of soap. She brought it to her cheek. She smiled. Then she put her head down on the canteen table and fell asleep, still holding his hand. He was still there when she woke up four hours later. His hand was numb, but he said nothing. She got up, stretched, yawning loudly. The canteen had closed. Apart from a cleaner pushing a mop reluctantly around the room, they were alone.

"I'm going to my room," she said, leaning over the table and kissing him lightly on the forehead.

He sat in the gathering darkness, rubbing the spot where she had kissed him.

Now

XXIX

Even for the dead.

Second chances are a fact of life for the Igbo. A person who lived poor and was buried poor can, when a relative makes enough money, receive a second burial. Full of the pomp and grandeur reserved for the rich. So even in death, in Hades, the dead one can get a chance to taste the wealth that eluded him in his previous incarnation, perhaps sweetening the deal for his next one.

Why did these people know nothing of this? Of the complexities of life and how you can never recapture the way a particular shaft of light, falling through a tree, patterned the floor in a shower of shadows. You just opened your heart because you knew tomorrow there would be another shaft of light, another tree, and another rain of shadows. Each particular. Not the same as yesterday's. Not as beautiful as yesterday's. Only as beautiful as today's.

Even the dead knew this.

Then

XXX

The police search of hospitals had so far failed to turn up anyone with a missing penis.

Weeks passed and Derek visited her every day in the hospital where she was being held, although it felt more like a correctional facility. She knew it was his job, but with time she liked to pretend that he was her friend and that he came to see her because he wanted to.

They did become friends and gradually she opened up to him, told him a little about her life. He tried to put the puzzle together. Mother died during childbirth. Child probably abused by successive male relatives, ran away from home one night clutching that terrible legacy. Not uncommon. But no matter how hard he pressed, the memory of Mary's eyes at the door on the first night of her rape kept Abigail from telling him or the police where to find Peter.

Derek's colleagues recommended psychiatric treatment

in a confined facility, but he fought them. He didn't believe she was crazy. Meanwhile, the search for her parents turned up nothing. Even the name she gave, Abigail Tansi, drew a blank. It was like she didn't exist. And she didn't, because Peter had used a fake passport and a forged visa to bring her into the country and she was registered everywhere under that fake name, a name she had forgotten.

She was a ghost.

Now

XXXI

The comfort of simple things.

Coffee percolating. Cinnamon buns warming oven and home. An ice-cold Coca-Cola on a hot day. Licking out the mixing bowl. Chocolate.

Childhood.

It was perhaps the one thing Abigail had never really had, and yet truly needed. Yet somehow, to be nostalgic in this way for a thing never experienced.

Not that anyone was to blame, she thought, blowing smoke rings that dissipated before they were quite formed. These things just happen. *Ije uwa,* as the Igbos would say. One's walk in this life. Interesting that the Igbo don't believe the path to be fixed, or even problematic. Destiny isn't a deck of cards stacked up against you. It is the particular idiosyncrasies of the player, not the deck or the dealer, that hold the key. Personality always sways the outcome of the game.

She stubbed out the cigarette on the broad concrete balustrade she was leaning on, the ash-heavy tip drawing strange lines and squiggles. Random.

The memory.

Myth, yet still truer than any lie.

An old woman her father took her to. A witch. To exorcize this devil of a longing in her, his daughter. This longing for death and the ways of the dead. A wanton melancholy that was a deep wound keeping her from life. The old woman's song that day that wasn't a day but a dream:

The mind is a bag, we each wear it differently. A palm can contain a star and yet we search for nothing. Here, child. Here. This is the heart.

And then, cutting strange lines and squiggles with a knife tip in the soot-covered earth by her hearth, sang on.

The heart is a cut. If there is only one opening, it grows wide and we die. Here I cut many openings, child. More than fifty. Straight and wavy. You will bleed many joys, child. How do you say to a bird, there is no more singing? Feed it a peppercorn.

Then plunging the knife into the flames licking the hearth's edge, she brought it up and cut Abigail twice on the face. On the left side, a straight line. On the right, a wave. Less than an inch long. Enough to break the skin, the hot metal cauterizing. Then laughing, she asked Abigail's father to buy Abigail some jewelry. A bracelet. Some earrings.

Absently rubbing her finger along the two lines on her face, the only marks on her body she hadn't cut herself, she wondered what happened to that jewelry.

She thought of her father hanging from a ceiling. The taut rope cutting the world into two: the moment before life and the moment before death. And in that rope, she wondered, was there the memory of her mother?

And what would be the line for her?

Derek?

Abigail?

A line is a lie. Who can tell what it will open onto?

Then

XXXII

It was Molly. It was Derek's wife.

And how many kingdoms had been lost for sugar? Or taken. The English knew all about that. About the slavery of desire. And so it was that the cocoa that Derek made to help Molly sleep, not sweet enough, led her downstairs.

Before death. And certainly before hell, there is always descent. Going. Down. Then death. And hell. Hardly a breath apart.

Turning the knob, opening. The door, opening. And there was Abigail, rump on the edge of the kitchen table, skirt up around her waist, naked breasts rubbing pert lines of sweat up and down Derek's chest, ankles locked around his back. Lost in the hot damp of Abigail: Derek. And over his shoulder, the women locked eyes. Abigail smiled.

Then Molly's scream. The stab. The look. Death. The look and the collapse onto the linoleum floor. Soft. Slow.

Just as Abigail would have imagined it. An autumn leaf. Falling. Cocoa, like old blood, spilling down the front of Molly's pale blue dressing gown. Rusting. Derek. Turning. Seeing his wife falling, even as his hips still jerked their urgent need. Then his mouth opened to call her name, screamed "Abigail!" instead, as he exploded into her.

Before he could pull up his trousers, Molly was gone.

Running down the street. Night. Late. Dressing gown stained with the bleeding of her pain. And then the police later. Derek looked cowed. Molly shamed, perhaps a little regretful. Abigail fought the blanket and the policewoman wrapping it around her. Fought the annihilation she could feel coming. The cold steel around Derek's wrists wrapping themselves around her heart.

"Hush, my love," he said. "Hush."

Then night and rain. And the policewoman soothing her: *There, there.*

In her room. Back at the hospital. Still raining. In the distance, Nina Simone on some cleaner's radio. *I put a spell on you.* In the distance.

Had her mother known this particular pain?

It didn't seem possible. More likely that she was becoming herself, this Abigail. In this particular moment, in this particular way. As particular as the dots burning across her body, mapping a constellation.

Now

XXXIII

Revenge is a raven.

Feathers blackened from hate. And Molly was relentless in her pursuit. Shame turning to the certainty of faith.

The reprisals were swift.

Derek was fired from his job and brought up on charges for the abuse of a minor. Nothing Abigail did helped. Her impassioned denial. Her letter saying it was her fault. Her choice. But they said they were doing this to protect her. That she didn't know what choice was. But she did. She who had been taken and taken and taken. And now the one time she took for herself, the one time she had choice in the matter, it was taken away. Maybe, she thought, maybe some of us are just here to feed others.

She struck match after match, watching their brief phosphorous flare. No, she thought, maybe I am not here as food, but to live for one phosphorous moment. No, she thought, bringing the flame of the last match to the tip of a cigarette, maybe I just light the fuse of my own destruction.

Forbidden to see or speak to Derek, she could only watch, heart on fire, as his disgrace was finalized publicly. Unable to comfort him, to take the look from his eyes when she saw him in court. The shame and the blame. No, she wanted to scream, no, my love, my heart. This was my choice. Damn this world, she thought, though she didn't really blame anyone. Things were just the way they were. Besides, how does a hunter tell a vegetarian lion from the rest? This time a peppercorn will not suffice.

And the social worker who bumped into her in the hall-way of the court as she watched Derek dragged away to await sentencing. Guilty. Guilty. Thin-lipped and angry, the woman bumped into her, and looking from Abigail to Derek and back, and mistaking the anguished look on Abigail's face, said to her: Don't you worry, sister, that monster is going away for a long time. And then the anguished look on the social worker's face as Abigail's not inconsiderable right hook connected with her nose.

Looking down at the terrified woman, she licked the blood on her knuckles.

But even that sacrifice hadn't been enough. It was just like the Igbo said. The sacrifice is always commensurate to the thing wished for. Sometimes a lizard will do, sometimes a goat, or a dog, sometimes a cow or buffalo. Sometimes, a human being.

That day, she knew she would never see Derek again. But

her love was the full measure of her decision.

As she blew smoke into night and the river, she knew, this decision was hard.

Now

XXXIV

A lie always sounds better told in English, her people said.

The heart knows the truth of this betrayal. The wish, the courage, it all falls away before the heart's lie. The realization that she could not live without Derek was not as sudden and surprising as her difficulty in the face of this task. Here she was trying to find the strength to save him.

She looked down at the river, then at the cigarette. A tug sounded its foghorn and the wind picked up. With a sigh she flicked the stub at the darkness and followed it.

Acknowledgements

Blair Holt, who never lets me be less than the artist I am sometimes afraid to be. Percival Everett, to whom nothing is inconceivable. Cristina Garcia, Aimee Bender, Steve Isoardi and Jeannette Lindsay, Ron Gottesman, PB Rippey, Johnny Temple, Johanna Ingalls, Kate Gale, Andrea Tuch, Parissa Ebrahimzadeh, Peter Orner, Douglas Humble, Johanna Parker, and Kristen Bonkemeyer.

The first finished draft of this book was completed in Marfa, Texas, while on a very generous Lannan Foundation Writers Residency. Thank you for always supporting and believing.

And Yvonne Vera, whose words are sublime: May You Rest In Peace.

If I have forgotten to list you here, forgive me, but please accept my thanks.

Also from **AKASHIC BOOKS**

JOHN CROW'S DEVIL by Marlon James
232 pages, hardcover, $19.95

"A powerful first novel . . . Writing with assurance
and control, James uses his small-town drama to
suggest the larger anguish of a postcolonial
Jamaican society struggling for its own identity."
—*New York Times*

"*Pile them up*, a Marlon James character says
repeatedly and Marlon does just that. Pile them up:
language, imagery, technique, imagination. All
fresh, all exciting. This is a good book and a writer
to watch out for."
—Chris Abani

SPEAK NOW by Kaylie Jones
300 pages, trade paperback, $14.95

"Perceptive, gritty, and compelling, this is an
absorbing book that dives headfirst into issues facing recovering addicts . . . Beautifully written and
richly detailed, it is highly recommended."
—*Library Journal*

LIMBO by Sean Keith Henry
270 pages, trade paperback, $15.95

"*Limbo* is a smart, honest novel about displace-
ment and the meaning of home. It struggles in turn
with the embracing of identity and the welcome
comfort of escape."
—PERCIVAL EVERETT

ABOUT THE AUTHOR

Christopher Pike is a bestselling author of young adult novels. The Thirst series, *The Secret of Ka*, and the Remember Me and Alosha trilogies are some of his favorite titles. He is also the author of several adult novels, including *Sati* and *The Season of Passage*. Thirst and Alosha are slated to be released as feature films. Pike currently lives in Santa Barbara, where it is rumored he never leaves his house. But he can be found online at christopherpikebooks.com.